THE MYSTERY AT

GRIZZLY GRAVEYARD

by Carole Marsh

Published by Gallopade International/Carole Marsh Books.
Printed in the United States of America.

First Edition ©2014 Carole Marsh/Gallopade International/Peachtree City, GA
Current Edition ©January 2015
Ebook edition ©2014
All rights reserved.
Manufactured in Peachtree City, GA

Managing Editor: Janice Baker
Assistant Editor: Susan Walworth
Cover and Content Design: John Hanson

Gallopade is proud to be a member and supporter of these educational organizations and associations:

American Booksellers Association
American Library Association
International Reading Association
National Association for Gifted Children
The National School Supply and Equipment Association
Museum Store Association
Association of Partners for Public Lands
Association of Booksellers for Children

Once upon a time …

Hmm, kids keep asking me to write a mystery book. What shall I do?

Mimi

Papa said …

Why don't you set the stories in real locations?

That's a great idea! And if I do that, I might as well choose real kids as characters in the stories! But which kids would I pick?

We can go on the *Mystery Girl* airplane ...

I can FLY US anYWHeRe!

Mystery Girl

Or aboard the *Mimi!*

Mimi

Take me to the Forbidden City!

Or by surfboard, rickshaw, motorbike, camel ...!

I can put a lot of **history, mystery, science,** legend, lore, and **laughs** in the books! It will be educational and fun!

Good stuff!

And so, join Mimi, Papa, Christina, Grant, Avery, Ella, Evan, and Sadie aboard the *Mystery Girl*—where the adventure is real and so are the characters!

START YOUR ADVENTURE TODAY!

READ THE BOOK!

GO ONLINE!

MEET THE CHARACTERS!

TRACK YOUR ADVENTURES!

www.carolemarshmysteries.com

IT WAS A GRIZZLY AFFAIR

When Papa and I went to Yellowstone National Park recently, we entered through the West Yellowstone gate. It was late September and we were excited to think that we might actually spy a grizzly bear once we got into the wilds of the park...but we didn't have to wait that long! We spotted the sign for the Grizzly & Wolf Discovery Center and took time to visit. We were so glad we did! We saw grizzlies galore! Many of them had been orphaned as cubs and had grown up at the center. They were humongous! Guess the name of one of them—my oldest grandson's name, Grant!

This was a very educational place to visit with all kinds of exhibits, live grizzlies and wolves on exhibit in a very natural habitat, and much more. But our favorite thing to witness was the grizzlies hunting for hidden food which the keepers had put beneath enormous logs and boulders. Those grizzlies were hungry, so they got busy using their hunting skills to find their lunch. I think they also enjoyed looking at us as much as we loved watching them. Since it was very cold, they probably wondered where all our "fur" was!

Enjoy learning about grizzlies in my brand-new mystery—if you can "bear" the suspense, scares, and surprises!

— *Carole Marsh*

1

GRIZZLY OR GHOST?

Ella spun round and round, eyeing the towering lodgepole pines through her camera lens. They surrounded her like playground bullies. The ashy-brown bark of their tall trunks was as scaly as alligator hide. Their branches, fluffy with green pine needles, formed Christmas-tree shapes high above her head.

When she had started down the narrow, dusty trail from the cabin, just outside the boundary of Yellowstone National Park, the lanky pines stood only here and there, offering friendly waves in the gentle autumn breeze. Eager to use her new camera, Ella imagined the tall pine trees were encouraging her to keep walking—to see what was just around the next curve. It was her first trip to this unspoiled wilderness, and she wanted to see it all—majestic mountains to **pristine** prairies, gurgling geysers to mysterious mud pots.

Ella was overjoyed when her grandparents, Mimi and Papa, invited her, her older sister Avery, and her younger brother Evan, to join them on a vacation to the famous park. Mimi even surprised Ella with her first real camera. "Every young sleuth needs a camera," Mimi told her. Sleuth was the word Mimi used instead of detective.

Mimi was a famous writer who always wrote about kids who stumbled into a mystery only to get tangled up in trouble like flies in a spider's web. But recently, she couldn't think of anything to write. "I need **inspiration**," she'd said, "and I know I can find it in Yellowstone!"

A sudden gust of wind sent the reddish-brown pine needles that carpeted the ground swirling around Ella's feet. She looked frantically in every direction. Where was the path that had led her into this piney grove?

All the trees looked the same! Ella knew Papa would describe them as "thicker than the hair on a grizzly bear's back!"

"Grizzlies!" Ella whispered. Her mind raced back to the pictures she'd seen of the massive furry animals that are known to live in Yellowstone. Her legs began to tremble. She wished she'd gone shopping with Mimi instead of wandering so far from the cabin. She hadn't even left Papa a note! And it had never occurred to her to mark the trail, or do something, *anything,* that would help her find her way back!

"I hope I don't become the inspiration for Mimi's next book," Ella muttered. "It could be *The Mystery of the Missing Granddaughter*, or *The Mystery of the Granddaughter Who Got in Big Trouble with Her Grandparents*!"

Another gust of wind, harder than the one before, made the pines creak and shake their shaggy heads. Ella's long blond hair twisted in the rowdy air before flopping across her face. She quickly pushed the unruly strands out of her eyes. Mimi always said, "Get your hair out of your eyes so you can see where you're going!" She just wished she knew which way to go.

Ella imagined the trees were laughing at the foolish girl standing in their shadows. Suddenly, she heard a mournful cry, like the moan of a ghost, drifting through the trees. Ella's fear turned to terror!

2

OLD GEEZER GEYSER

Mimi peeked through the cabin window. She spied Papa stretched out in a big armchair in the corner. A paperback Western novel rode up and down on his chest with each vibrating snore. She put her finger to her lips. "Shhh," she told Avery and Evan. "Let's surprise him!"

They tiptoed into the cabin they had rented near the small town of West Yellowstone, Montana. A few glowing coals remained from the fire Papa and the kids had built that morning before Mimi borrowed Papa's truck to drive to Livingston, Montana, for "supplies." Papa knew that "supplies" was Mimi's code word for "big-time shopping."

"I can't wait to tell Ella about our shopping trip," Avery whispered. Mimi peeked into one of her massive shopping bags. "I just hope the boots we bought fit her," she replied.

"Let's wake up Papa Yellowstone style!" Evan whispered excitedly. He raised his hands into the air like the claws of a grizzly bear.

Avery and Mimi joined Evan as he crept closer to Papa's chair. Evan giggled as he watched his grandfather sleeping. Papa breathed deeply, a loud snore rumbling from his throat, and then he spewed out the air like Yellowstone's famous geyser, Old Faithful.

Silently, Mimi mouthed a countdown of one, two, three. "GRRRRRRR!!!!!" they all roared.

Papa jumped up so fast that his book flew into the air and hit the ceiling. It flapped back down like a wounded bird before collapsing to the floor.

"Golly geysers!" Papa exclaimed.

Evan laughed so hard his side hurt. "That's a perfect choice of words, Papa!" he exclaimed. "You were erupting after every snore!"

Papa grinned sheepishly. "Guess that makes me a geezer geyser!" he said. "Why did you all scare me like that? You know we're smack dab in the middle of bear country. I thought a grouchy grizzly had climbed through the window to take my chair for his nap!"

"Sorry, Papa!" Avery said. She wrapped her arms around his neck. "I don't think you're an old geezer. You're my cowboy Papa!"

"Now that's the kind of bear hug I prefer!" Papa said.

Avery pecked Papa on the cheek, then grabbed her lips in pain. "Papa, you may not be a geezer, but you do feel a little like a grizzly. I think you need a shave!"

"An old cowpoke like me needs a big, bushy beard out here in the wide open spaces," Papa drawled in his deep voice. "Besides, winter's on its way and a nice beard will keep my face warm!"

Mimi frowned. "If you plan on looking like an old bear, you better go hibernate!" she said.

Avery grabbed the shopping bags. "We got you something better than a beard!"

she said, and plopped a big square box in Papa's lap.

"Nothin's gonna jump out of here, is it?" Papa asked. He gingerly opened the box and placed his hand inside. "It feels kind of furry in there!"

"They're hiking boots," Evan explained. "That fur around the top helps keep you warm."

"They sure are nice," Papa said, inspecting one of the brown lace-up boots. "But you know I always wear cowboy boots."

"Cowboy boots are good for riding horses," Mimi said. "For all the walking we'll be doing, you need hiking boots. Yellowstone National Park is more than 3,400 square miles, you know."

"Hold it right there, Mimi," Avery said, pulling her smartphone out of her back pocket. Her fingers moved quickly over the screen. "Did you know that 3,400 square miles is more than 2 million acres?"

"I didn't know that exactly," Mimi said, "but I do know that Yellowstone is about the size of the states of Delaware and Rhode Island combined!"

"I have trouble with those itty bitty states," Evan chimed in. "They're not even big enough to write their names inside. Every time I have a map test, I have to write their names in the Atlantic Ocean."

"OK, OK," Papa said. "I get it. Yellowstone is one of the largest national parks in the country, and I know I need hiking boots. I'll wear 'em as long as I can wear my cowboy hat with 'em." He gave a quick wink to Avery and Evan before adding, "...and I get to keep my beard."

Mimi pulled on the hiking boots she was lucky enough to find in red, her favorite color. "I sure hope grizzlies are color blind," she said. "If not, they can spot me coming from a mile away."

"No, they're not," Avery remarked. "I just finished a book about them. They see colors very well."

"Well, they'll just know what great fashion sense I have," Mimi declared.

"I can't wait to show Ella the boots we got for her," Avery told Papa.

"Yeah!" Evan agreed. "The sales lady took off a person's age!"

Papa looked confused.

"No, Evan," Avery said. "She took off a percentage. The boots were originally $85. Mimi only paid $59.50." She pulled out her phone again and opened her calculator app. "That's 30 percent off," she explained proudly.

"Good job, Avery," Mimi said. "STEM sure comes in handy."

Papa looked confused. "What in the world are you talking about?" he asked.

"Mimi's talking about Science, Technology, Engineering, and Math," Avery explained. "It's what kids are learning in school these days. That's the second time I've used the math part in the last few minutes!"

"And the technology," Mimi added, pointing to Avery's phone. "We didn't even use calculators when I was in school!"

Avery searched through the bags and pulled out Ella's boots. "Where is Ella?" she asked Papa.

"She must be napping in the bunkroom," Papa said. "She was reading the instruction booklet for her camera when I dozed off."

"Let's scare her like we did Papa," Evan suggested, posing his "claws" in the air. "Grrrrrrrr!" he growled and headed down the hallway.

When they reached the bunkroom, they saw that all the bunks were still neatly made with bedspreads covered with pictures of wild horses, tumbleweeds, and howling coyotes. Ella was nowhere to be found.

"Ella?" Evan called to his sister.

Avery knew her little sister's curiosity often got her into trouble. She also knew that big animals with sharp teeth lived in this part of Montana. She felt a little worried knot tighten up in her belly.

"She's not here!" Avery shouted back to Mimi and Papa. "Ella's missing!"

Evan acting like a bear!

3

TALKING BONE

Ella stood frozen in the grove of pines. The mournful moan rose and fell on the wind. It seemed to come from every direction, echoing among the trees. Ella noticed the shadows were growing longer. Soon, it would be dusk. Her thoughts bounced like ping-pong balls. *Should I run? But I don't know which way to go! Should I stand like a statue? I hope Mimi and Papa find me before a ghost does, or worse—a bear!*

Before Ella could decide what to do, another strange sound ripped through the trees. It was a high-pitched cry, like that of a scared woman, but it sounded sad. Ella's feet didn't wait for a decision—her blue sneakers took off running!

The trees grew thicker and thicker, and soon the thorny branches of undergrowth were clawing at Ella's clothes. The cry followed her. Ella glanced over her shoulder, but before she could see anything, her foot caught on something on the ground. She sprawled across the forest floor.

Another cry rang out and Ella scrambled like a lizard behind a small boulder. Huddled behind it, gasping for breath, she heard the soft, padded sound of galloping footsteps behind her. The footsteps grew closer, slowed, and paused from time to time. The crying stopped, but it was replaced by huffing, grunting sounds. Ella clasped her hands over her head and squeezed her eyes shut. If she didn't see whatever it was, maybe it wouldn't see her.

Suddenly, something click-clacked on the rock. Ella felt hot, steamy breath on her hands. It was right above her head! With nowhere else to run, Ella wasn't about to give up without a fight. She jumped up, waving her hands wildly in the air. To her surprise, she didn't see a ghost or a man-eater! In fact it looked a lot like her favorite teddy bear!

A bear cub, startled by her commotion, slid down the rock and stared in bewilderment. He was about the size of their family dog, Clue, except much rounder and fatter. His half-moon ears barely stuck above his plush fur.

"Hello there, little fellow," Ella said gently. She remembered Mimi's words— "Never touch wild animals, no matter how friendly or cute."

The bear cub sniffed closer and let out the same mournful cry Ella heard earlier. "I didn't mean to scare you!" Ella said, slowly backing away. "Are you lost, too? You better run along. Your mom's probably looking for you." But the cub only blinked his big brown eyes at her.

"I know you're not supposed to talk to strangers," Ella continued in the same voice she used when talking with her baby sister, Sadie, who wasn't yet old enough to come on adventures with Mimi and Papa. "So I'll just talk to you. I certainly hope someone's looking for me by now. I sure am ready to see my family, even my pesky little brother."

Ella knew the most dangerous time to be around a mama grizzly was when her cubs were nearby. As cute as the little fella was, she didn't want big, mad mama to find her babysitting. She reached down for her camera. If she couldn't touch him, at least she could take a picture. How else would anyone believe she'd had a conversation with a baby grizzly?

"Oh no! Where's my camera?" Ella said. She patted down her side where the camera hung before her sprint through the trees. "The strap must have snagged on something and snapped," she decided. She looked around, and a glint of white caught her eye. She leaned into the last rays of sunlight and plucked the white object from the ground.

It looks like some kind of bone, Ella thought, turning it in her hand. She thought about the ghostly sounds she had heard in the trees. *Could these bones be from whatever made that sound?* A shudder crawled up her spine like a centipede. She knew that bones could say a lot, if the right person listened.

4

RESCUE RANGER

The bear cub cautiously crept closer to Ella. She watched, puzzled, as he stuck his nose in the air and sniffed wildly. Could he smell the creeping darkness? She shivered again. Sure, it was getting colder fast, but the shivers running down her spine were not from the cold, but from concern that the dark night would soon find her lost in the woods, far from her family. *Mimi and Papa will find me,* she thought. *I know they will.*

The cub seemed as nervous as Ella, and although the cub was careful not to get too close to her, he showed no interest in leaving. "We'll watch out for each other," she told the cub. "I'm glad you're here with me." She studied the bone once more. *What happened to the poor creature? Did the same fate await her?*

Ella removed her blue scarf from around her neck. It was the one Papa had given her because he said it matched her eyes. She wrapped the bone in the scarf and tucked it inside the pocket of her jacket so the bone wouldn't jab her. Then, she zipped her jacket, tucked her knees underneath it, and leaned against the rock to brave the frigid night ahead.

She remembered her science lesson on heat and wished she had worn her heavy coat. It would be a much better **insulator,** not letting the heat from her body escape into the air. She looked at the cub's dense fur and knew he'd be cozy in the cold—fur was an excellent insulator. The rock felt cold through her jacket. If the rock had been in a clearing, it would have absorbed the heat from the sun and would have been a good **conductor** of that heat. But unfortunately, the trees had kept the sun's rays from reaching it.

Ella began to softly hum *Polly Wolly Doodle*. Mimi had taught her the song, and they'd sung it several times during their long drive out west. Ella hoped it would help calm her fear. The little bear pricked his ears at her and soon lay down on the ground like a baby who desperately needed a nap.

After Ella sang what must have been the tenth chorus, the little bear sprang back to his feet and peered into the darkness. Then, Ella heard it, too. Something was plowing through the brush. "It must be mama bear!" Ella whispered fearfully. She jumped to her feet, ready to run.

"ELLLLLAAAAA! ELLLLAAAAA!" Flashlight beams pierced the darkness. "Papa!" she yelled. "I'm here, Papa!"

She clambered on top of the rock and crossed her arms back and forth over her head. "Over here!" she called.

"Forgot to leave a trail of breadcrumbs, didn't you?" Papa said, pulling Ella off the rock and into a hug.

"I'm sorry, Papa!" Ella sobbed with relief into her grandfather's shoulder. "I didn't mean to get lost!"

"You can apologize later," Papa said. "Right now, I'm so happy to see you I could squeeze the stuffin' out of you!"

Once Papa put her back on the ground, Ella noticed he wasn't alone. Two people stood behind him—her older sister, Avery, and a man in a green uniform. Avery scanned the ground with the flashlight app on her phone, while the man spoke to Mimi on his cell phone.

"She's fine, ma'am," he said. "We'll have her back to you soon, safe and sound."

Papa introduced the man to Ella once he was off the phone with Mimi. "This is Ranger Warren," Papa explained. "Mimi and Evan are waiting in the truck. We were out looking for you when we spotted him. I don't think we would have found you without his help."

"Thank you," Ella said. "I'm sorry for all the trouble I've caused."

"I'm just thankful this little mystery has a happy ending," Ranger Warren said. "Yellowstone is no place for a little girl to explore alone."

"You mean we're inside the park?" Ella said.

"Yes," Papa answered. "You walked more than two miles from our cabin!"

"Wow!" Ella said. "Of course, I probably *ran* the second mile, before I ran into him."

Avery grabbed her sister in a big hug, then pushed back. "You said 'him.' Who was with you?" she asked Ella.

"Just that little cub," Ella replied. She pointed toward the rock, but the cub was gone.

Papa and Avery, who knew Ella had a vivid imagination, looked even more confused.

"Your mind can play tricks on you when you're in the forest alone," Ranger Warren said quickly.

"But he was here!" Ella insisted. "He was just as real as all of you!"

"I'll report your sighting," the ranger said. "If he's an orphan, maybe they'll take him in at the Grizzly & Wolf Discovery Center in West Yellowstone. It's a place for bears and wolves that can no longer live in the wild."

As Papa thanked the ranger once more, Avery motioned for Ella to come near. "I don't think bear tracks would look like this," she whispered. She aimed her flashlight app back at the strange oval marks about a foot long. "It might not be a bear track," she added softly, "but someone or some *thing* made these tracks!"

5

CABIN CATASTROPHE

"Why can't I see a bear cub?" Evan wailed as Papa started up the truck to head back to the cabin. "It's not fair that Ella found a bear cub, and I can't even see it!"

"Maybe we can see him tomorrow," Mimi said, "if the rangers find him."

"Yes," Papa agreed. "We had already planned to visit the Grizzly & Wolf Discovery Center to learn about local wildlife—especially grizzlies—before we venture into Yellowstone. Besides, it's getting late. I'm ready to hibernate, at least for the night!"

"I hope they find him and take good care of him," Ella said. "He looked so lost and afraid."

"Sort of like you," Papa said.

"Yeah," Avery agreed, "but you're not as cute as a cub!"

Ella stuck out her tongue at Avery.

"Dare you to do that again," Avery said, reaching into her coat pocket.

Ella stuck her tongue out even farther than she had the first time and crossed her eyes.

FLASH! Avery snapped a picture.

"My camera!" Ella said. "Where'd you find it?"

"I saw it hanging on a bush," Avery said. "It was like a clue. That's how we knew we were on the right path to find you!"

"I guess my camera helped save my life!" Ella exclaimed.

Mimi put her arm around Ella's shoulders and smiled. "I told you every great sleuth needs a camera!"

Papa pulled the truck into the dirt driveway of their rustic log cabin, which was now bathed in soft, white moonlight. Evan grabbed Papa's keys and ran ahead to unlock the cabin door. He fumbled with the lock until it finally clicked. When he pushed the door open, however, he quickly turned back to them with a shocked expression.

"I didn't do it!" he yelled, shaking his head so hard that his blonde hair stood straight out from his head.

The sight that met them all was beyond belief. The cabin looked like a tornado had blown through it. Tables and chairs were flipped on their sides. Cabinet doors hung wide open. One of them was torn completely off and lay on the floor.

Crunch! Crunch! Crunch! Papa's footsteps sounded like he was walking on gravel as he stepped on cereal pieces strewn across the floor. The ripped-open boxes lay helter-skelter around the room.

Evan clapped his hands to his cheeks. "What will I eat for breakfast tomorrow?" he asked, exasperated.

"That's the least of our worries," Mimi said, eyeing the deep scratches on the front of the refrigerator.

"Grrrroooossssss!" Ella cried. She pointed to a jar of mayonnaise in the middle of the kitchen floor. Inside the jar, dirty flecks were mixed in the mayo like black pepper on mashed potatoes.

"Let me see," Evan said as he looked into the jar. PLOP! A big glob of gooey, greasy mayo stuck to the ceiling suddenly let go and splatted on Evan's head.

Avery and Ella giggled uncontrollably. "Do you think this mess is funny?" Evan scolded them. "How'd that get up there, anyway?" he added, as he stuck his finger in the glob to taste it.

"When the jar was dropped or knocked to the floor, the force of the impact **propelled** the mayo up," Avery said. "The pull of gravity brought it back down." Avery snickered at her brother again. "Gravity has great timing!"

"Very funny!" Evan said with a disgusted smirk.

"Don't worry, little brother," Avery said. "Mayonnaise is a great hair conditioner. Those blonde locks of yours will be **lustrous**!"

"Well, I think the people who broke in here and did this to our cabin are pigs!" Evan said.

Mimi shook her head and picked up one of the overturned kitchen chairs made from logs. "I think you've got the wrong fairy tale," she said. "This reminds me a lot more of *Goldilocks and the Three Bears!*"

"Yeah," Avery agreed. "But unfortunately nothing was 'just right.'"

"I'm checking the beds," Evan said as he ran to the bedrooms. "They're torn to pieces!" he yelled back.

Papa picked up a door knob still attached to a piece of splintered wood, and walked to the back of the cabin. "They broke in through the back door," he said, "but nothing seems to be missing. It's too late to do anything tonight, so I'll notify the park rangers first thing in the morning. For now, I'll get the camping gear out of the truck and we'll do some indoor camping tonight. Then I'll put the door back together so that whatever broke in here can't get back inside!"

"Awesome!" Evan said. "Can we get a fire going again in the fireplace and make some s'mores?"

"I'm afraid you'd have to pick up the ingredients off the floor," Mimi said.

"Oh, yeah," Evan said. "I forgot that all our food is wrecked."

The tent went up quickly and almost as soon as Mimi and Papa had zipped their sleeping bags, both of them were snoring soundly.

As exhausted as she was, Ella couldn't sleep. She needed to tell Avery and Evan about the spooky noises, about meeting the bear cub, and especially about the strange bone. She certainly didn't want to concern Mimi and Papa any more than she already had. After all, Mimi had come to Yellowstone for relaxation and inspiration, not worry and exasperation.

"Are you sure you didn't imagine that bear cub?" Avery whispered.

"No!" Ella replied. "I pinky promise he was for real—just as real as this thing I found in the woods." She unrolled her scarf and showed them the bone.

Evan's eyes grew wide. "OOOH! For once in my life, I'm glad I went shopping!" he said.

"Wait a minute," Avery said. She reached for Ella's camera and flipped through the pictures. The screen cast an eerie glow across her face. "When I was looking at the funny picture I made of you, I saw something weird," she said. "Did you see only one bone back in the forest?"

"Yes," Ella said, "but it was getting dark."

Avery passed the camera to her. "How do you explain this?"

Ella couldn't believe her eyes. The photograph showed a blurred shot of the ground. Papa would have called it catawampus. In it was part of a pine tree with a twisted knot on its side. Scattered amongst the pine straw were unusual, white objects.

"Those look like bones!" Ella whispered excitedly. "But I don't remember making that shot! I must have hit the shutter accidentally when I was running!"

Evan leaned over and peered at the picture. "Sure looks like bones to me," he said. "Do you think it could be a graveyard?"

6

A LITTLE BIRD TOLD ME

Tweeeet! Tweet! Tweeeet! Tweet! "Somebody turn off that alarm clock!" Evan grumbled. He rolled over in his sleeping bag and pulled it over his ears.

The commotion woke Avery too. "Oh, how cute!" she said.

"I know I'm cute!" Evan mumbled. "But I need more sleep. Quit tapping me!"

"I'm not tapping you," Avery said. "There's a little bird hopping around on your sleeping bag!"

"No way I'm falling for that one," Evan said.

"What's going on?" Mimi said. She peeled back her red sleeping bag and yawned.

Avery pointed at the little bird. It turned its head left and right, looking at them like they were the most fascinating creatures it had ever seen. Tweeeet! Tweet! Tweeeeet!

Mimi, who enjoyed learning about each and every bird that visited her backyard birdfeeder, recognized this one. "That's a black-capped chickadee," she said. "He must have seen the open door and made himself at home. I'm amazed at how many different bird species you can see in the great outdoors. I've read that there are more than 300 bird species in Yellowstone Park!"

"The white under his chin looks like he's wearing a baby bib," Avery said.

"Well, it's too bad he's not wearing a diaper," Mimi quipped. "Looks like he left a good morning present on Evan's sleeping bag!"

"What!?" Evan bolted up, startling the little bird that flittered to the top of the tent trying to find a way out. "Why does everything have to land on me?" he asked.

Avery poked Ella's sleeping bag. "Ella, wake up! You've got to see this!"

When Ella didn't respond, Avery looked at her sister's sleeping bag. It was rumpled, but empty. Avery's heart somersaulted in her chest. "Not again!" she exclaimed.

"Everything's OK," Mimi said. She was reading something written on a scrap of paper. "Papa's gone, too, but he left a note. They left together early this morning to report the break-in."

The chickadee gave up trying to escape the tent and landed back on Evan's sleeping bag.

"He looks upset," Avery said. "I'll help him back outside." She threw back the tent flap and used her blanket to shoo the little bird out the back door.

Struck by the awesome view of the snow-capped mountains on the horizon, Avery stepped out of the cabin and wrapped the blanket around her shoulders. Her breath formed smoky little puffs in the crisp air. She had learned in science that the little clouds were not really made of smoke. Instead, they were formed from the water vapor in her breath changing from a gas to a liquid in the cold air. Still, it was fascinating, and Avery huffed out dragon puffs and watched them float away while she thought about the previous night's events. One mystery was too many, but now there were several. *Did Ella really see a cub in the woods? What made the strange footprints? Why were there bones in the woods? Who wrecked their cabin?*

The chickadee fluttered to a bare spot of ground and scratched and pecked furiously. Avery walked over to see what he was up to, and he immediately flew away. She couldn't see what the bird was eating, but she saw something much more interesting. Four footprints were visible, each with five toes. They looked like they came from someone walking on tippy toes. "Why would someone want to go barefoot in this cold weather?" she said to herself.

Strangely, the footprints didn't lead anywhere. It was as if whoever made them had hopped once on the ground and disappeared.

Avery kept looking. Nearby, she found more of the same odd oval marks she had seen in the forest where they found Ella. *Had something followed them here? Had it destroyed their cabin? If so, why?*

Feeling her toes growing numb, Avery realized she had walked outside wearing only socks. She made a step and noticed that wearing thick socks kept her foot from making a detailed footprint. *Interesting,* she thought, still wondering about the strange oval prints.

She twirled on her heels to scamper back inside, but a scrap of paper trapped in the branches of shrub caught her eye. Avery snatched the crumpled card before the wind picked it up. It was ripped in half, but she could tell it had once been a business card, like the ones Mimi had that said *MYSTERY WRITER* on them.

One side of the card had letters with other letters worn away. All she could make out was part of two words, "Wild" and "Rem," The other side of the paper had a handwritten message scratched in pen:

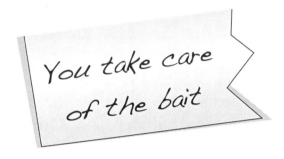

You take care
of the bait

Avery wasn't sure what the prints or the note meant, but she felt the chickadee had repaid her for helping him out of the cabin. This card was one more clue to solving the tangle of mysterious events. She glanced up at the little bird and smiled. "Thanks!" she said.

7

REFRIGERATOR RAIDERS

Inside the chilly cabin, Mimi and Evan had already changed out of their pajamas, and Mimi had a fire roaring in the fireplace.

"My stomach's growling louder than a grizzly bear," Evan complained.

"Maybe you should go out and look for some wild berries," Avery suggested. She pulled off her damp socks and toasted her toes by the fire.

"Are you kidding me?" Evan said. "That's what grizzlies eat for breakfast! We might show up at the same bush!"

Before Avery could offer another suggestion, Papa and Ella marched through the rickety back door.

"Who's hungry?" Papa said. "I've got some fresh, hot donuts!"

"They're delicious!" Ella said.

"Let me guess," Mimi said, noticing the white powder around Ella's mouth. "You like the ones covered in powdered sugar."

"Yep!" Ella said. "And they have berry filling on the inside!"

"I'll take one of those," Evan said. "Berry-flavored donuts are the perfect breakfast for someone who's hungry as a bear!"

"Did you report our break-in?" Mimi asked.

"Luckily, we ran into Ranger Warren at the donut shop," Papa said. "He followed us here and is taking a look around outside."

Avery noticed that Papa was wearing his cowboy boots. "Why aren't you wearing your new hiking boots?" she asked.

"I couldn't find them anywhere this morning," he said. "Whoever broke into the cabin must have wandered off with my boots. Besides, I wasn't planning on hiking to the donut shop!"

Ranger Warren stepped inside just as Evan and Avery pulled apart the last donut in the box to share. The filling came out in a sticky blob and landed on Evan's knee. Avery giggled. Evan rolled his eyes, wiped it off his jeans with his finger, and swiped it across his tongue. "Lucky me!" he said. "I got all the filling. Looks like gravity was on my side this time. Thanks, gravity!"

Avery looked disgusted. "Lucky it wasn't bird poo!" she exclaimed.

Ella didn't laugh at Avery and Evan's antics. She immediately began peppering Ranger Warren with questions. "Did they find the cub?" she asked. "Is he OK? Where did they take him?"

"Whoa! Hold on," Ranger Warren said. "I haven't heard anything about your mysterious cub."

Mimi saw Ella's face fall. "Don't forget we're going to the Grizzly & Wolf Discovery Center," Mimi said. "Maybe they'll know something there."

Ella's face brightened. "Oh, that's right!" she said, remembering the plan.

"I guess you like powdered donuts, too," Avery said, pointing to the white powder on the ranger's pants leg.

The ranger smiled self-consciously before furiously brushing away the powder with his hand. He took off his hat, scratched his head, and surveyed the **shambles** of the cabin.

"I like your Smokey Bear hat," Evan said to Ranger Warren, recognizing the familiar headgear from when Smokey Bear had visited his school.

"Thanks," Ranger Warren said, running his hand around the brim. "Smokey actually works for the Forest Service, not the Park Service. He did borrow our hat, though. I guess Smokey would be really disappointed to know that some of his fellow bears did this to your cabin."

"You think bears did this?" Avery asked.

"No question about it," Ranger Warren said. "There was another cabin hit not too far from here. Luckily, no one was staying there. And I'm glad you folks were gone when your cabin was attacked."

"Yeah!" Evan exclaimed. "It's a good thing Ella got lost. Well, I mean it wasn't good, but..."

"We know what you mean, Evan," Mimi said.

"Papa!" Ella exclaimed. "That bear must have put on your boots and hiked away from our cabin!"

"That would be a sight to see, wouldn't it?" Papa said and chuckled.

"Bear break-ins are no laughing matter," Ranger Warren interrupted, "and this looks like a prime example, especially those claw marks on the refrigerator."

"Oh, did you see those?" Avery asked.

Ranger Warren looked at the ground and cleared his throat. Before he could answer, Evan piped in. "Did the bear break in just to raid our refrigerator?" he asked.

"Bears are especially hungry this time of year when they're preparing to hibernate, Evan," Mimi explained. "They need all the calories they can find to increase the body fat they live off of during hibernation."

"That's right," Avery said. "I read they can eat as much as 90 pounds a day!"

"Oh wow!" Evan said. "That's more than I weigh! At least that's more than I weighed before I ate all those donuts!"

"That's all true," Ranger Warren said. "But I don't know what's gotten into these bears around here. It seems that a lot of them are turning into **rogues**."

"Does that mean people are making house coats out of them?" Evan asked.

"No, Evan," Ella said, giggling. "He said rogues, not robes! Rogue animals don't act the way they should, and they do bad things."

Ranger Warren smiled. "Just like people who do bad things, bears have to be punished, too," he explained.

"Like being sent to 'bear time-out'?" Evan asked innocently.

"I'm afraid it's much more serious than that," the ranger explained. "Bears that break into cabins and eat people's food are not afraid of humans any longer. That makes them very dangerous. They usually have to be put to sleep."

"What about when they wake up?" Evan asked.

"By 'put to sleep,' he means they are killed," Mimi explained.

"I hope you don't mind, but I called the local newspaper to come out and take pictures," Ranger Warren said. "We need to warn others."

Ella thought about her little cub again. *Had talking to the cub made it lose its fear of humans? Would he grow up to become a rogue, too?*

Avery wondered if the cub, the bones, the weird footprints, the card, and the cabin catastrophe were related. *To get to the bottom of this mystery, she knew they'd need to dig deep into their bag of sleuthing skills.*

Evan, Ella, and Avery enjoy
eating donuts!

8

SCAT

"SCAT!" yelled a boy with shoulder-length hair blacker than ink.

Evan exited the building after a bathroom stop at the Grizzly & Wolf Discovery Center. He spun around, expecting to see a cat somewhere. After all, Mimi always said "Scat cat!" to scare the neighborhood cats off her porch.

"I don't see a cat anywhere," Evan said, curious.

But the boy shouted "Scat!" again as soon as Evan took his next step. "What is he talking about?" Evan asked, just as his foot SQUISHED into a pile of coffee-colored, smelly goo.

"I tried to warn you!" the boy said.

"Warn me about what?" Evan asked, wiping his hiking boot on the grass.

"The scat," he said, "also known as bear poop."

"Yuuuuuuck!" Evan said, wiping his shoe even harder. "You mean bear poop is called scat? I thought you were telling me to scat!"

"Well, if you had scatted you wouldn't have stepped in the scat," the boy replied.

Evan shook his head. It was too much for his brain to process.

"I'm Owen Cooper Joseph," the boy said, sticking his hand out to Evan for a shake. "You can tell a lot about a bear from his poop, you know." He raked through the scat with the edge of his shovel. "You can tell what the bear ate, whether or not it has parasites, where its **habitat** is—all kinds of things. This bear just ate some fish. See the bones?"

"How do you know so much about bear poop?" Evan asked, squeamishly looking at the fish bones sticking out of the scat.

"I hope to become a **wildlife biologist** some day," he said. "To learn everything I can, I volunteer here at the Center."

Evan nervously surveyed the area. "If there's bear poop here, there must be a bear nearby."

Owen grinned. "Yes, there are bears nearby," he said, "grizzlies that were becoming too comfortable around humans to live in the wild. That's part of the mission of this place—to teach humans what they can do to help the bears stay wild. But don't worry. All the bears here are safely contained. I'm afraid I dropped this bear scat when I was hauling it to the compost pile."

"There's a compost pile of bear poop?" Evan asked.

"Yes," Owen said. "We layer the scat with straw, grass clippings, and other natural wastes. **Microorganisms** help to break down the material to create compost, or humus."

"Yeah!" Evan said. "We learned about humus this year in school when we studied the types of soil. Dirt's not just dirt, you know!"

"I agree!" Owen said with a grin. "Composting is a way to recycle some of our waste here at the Grizzly & Wolf Discovery Center to keep it out of the landfill."

"I guess that's why there weren't any paper towels in the bathroom," Evan said.

"Yep," Owen said, leaning on the handle of his shovel. "The Center installed automatic hand dryers instead."

"I saw those," Evan said. "But I did something even better for the environment. I dried my hands on my pants. You don't need electricity for that!"

"There you are!" Ella said, trotting toward Evan, her camera bouncing at her side. "We thought you were lost in the bathroom."

She stopped and sniffed. "Wait a minute! Why does it smell like a dirty bathroom out here?"

Evan slapped his knee and laughed. "You just stepped in bear poop!"

"Looks like I've got to teach someone else about bear scat," Owen said.

Before Evan could introduce his new friend, Avery, Mimi, and Papa arrived. Evan was surprised to see a regal, black-and-white dog prancing amongst them. Its black tail curled over its back with a white point at the end like the period underneath a question mark.

"I've always wanted a dog like this!" Evan exclaimed, playfully ruffling the fur around the dog's neck. "Please say we can keep her!"

"Oh, you can't have her," Owen explained. He shoved his hand in his pocket and motioned for the dog to sit before giving her a treat. "She lives and works here at the Center. Her name is Jewel. She's a Karelian Bear Dog."

"How interesting!" Mimi said. "She did greet us like a goodwill **ambassador**!

"A bear dog?" Ella asked as she scraped the scat from the bottom of her new, cotton-candy-pink hiking boots.

"Karelian Bear Dogs are rare in the United States," Owen explained, "but in their homeland of Finland, they're national treasures. They're closely related to wolves. They were bred to hunt bears."

"Is Jewel a bear hunter?" Avery asked.

"Not exactly," Owen said. "As more and more people move into the western states, the bear's natural environment is disappearing. Bears wander into towns to find food. These rogue bears rummage in people's trash and sometimes even break into people's homes. Jewel is retired now, but she was part of a program that uses Karelian Bear Dogs to scare bears away from the areas where they might cause a problem with humans."

Evan kneeled and looked into Jewel's piercing, dark eyes. "Where were you when we needed you to keep those rascally bears out of our cabin?" he asked.

Owen cocked his head to one side and had a puzzled look on his face. "You had bears in your cabin?" he asked. "Are you staying in Cody, Wyoming?"

"No," Papa said, "right here in West Yellowstone."

Jewel put a halt to the conversation. She suddenly barked ferociously as a dark, furry creature stepped out of the shadows of a nearby building.

"Bear!" Evan yelled.

Karelian Bear Dog

9

BEAR ATTACK

Before anyone else had time to react, Evan sprinted away like an Olympic track star. Owen grabbed Jewel's collar and yelled, "It's OK! It's OK!" Jewel immediately calmed down and stopped barking. Ella quickly saw why.

The furry creature headed their way looked like a bear walking on its hind legs, but as it got closer, it was obvious that it wasn't a bear at all. It was a young man wearing a bearskin over his head and body.

"It's only Brad," Owen said reassuringly.

As the young man got closer, he flipped the bearskin off his head and Ella saw that he was blonde with a buzz cut.

"I see you're playing the role of the bear again today," Owen said.

"How'd you guess?" Brad said with a smirk.

"Evan!" Ella called for her brother, who peered cautiously at them from behind a flagpole. "You can come back now! This big bear won't hurt you."

"Brad is a student at the University of Montana," Owen said. "That's where I hope to go in a few years."

"I *was* a student," Brad corrected Owen. "Ran out of money. Can't go back until I earn more." He rubbed the bearskin with a disgusted look on his face. "That's why I'm doing this."

"Scaring visitors?" Evan asked, still trying to catch his breath.

"I've gotta have some fun with this awful job," Brad said.

"We have a program here that teaches people how to react if they see a bear," Owen explained.

"Brad plays the bear while a ranger teaches the audience how to react."

"So, how'd I do?" Evan asked.

"Horribly," Owen said. "You should never run when you see a bear! Bears are predators and when you run, they think of you as prey and try to catch you!"

"But I can run fast!" Evan said proudly.

Brad frowned. "Don't ever think you can outrun a bear. The human speed record is slightly less than 28 miles per hour. A bear can sprint at 35 miles per hour."

Avery quickly pulled out her phone and opened her calculator app.

"Miss Smartphone is at it again," Evan said. "She's a regular mathematician since she got that phone!"

Avery rolled her eyes at her brother and sighed. Her fingers went to work. "So, 28 is 80 percent of 35," she muttered as she did the calculations. "That means a bear is about 20 percent faster than a human!"

"Well, what *should* you do if you cross paths with a bear?" Ella asked. She remembered the strange sounds she heard in the woods and how she had run. She hoped she was never in that situation again, but just in case...

"First," Owen said, "let the bear know that you're a human. Talk to it in a calm voice and don't look it in the eye." He stuck out his arms. "Put your arms out to the side like this and wave them slowly up and down. Then, slowly walk backwards the way you came."

Brad flipped the bearskin back over his head and moved threateningly toward Owen.

"Then," Owen said, "if the bear charges at you, the best thing to do is to play dead."

Brad lunged at Owen, who dropped to the ground and covered his head and neck with his arms and hands. He lay silently as Brad pretended to claw at him.

Evan shuddered at the thought of a bear attack and was thankful they were gone when the bear broke into the cabin.

"The best thing," Owen said, "is to always carry bear spray with you when you're in bear country. You don't want to get **mauled** by a bear!"

"Don't you have some bear spray, Mimi?" Evan asked.

"No, Evan," Mimi said. "That's my *hair* spray, not *bear* spray."

"Bear spray is made from hot peppers," Owen said. "It irritates the bear's eyes, nose, throat, and lungs so badly that it disables them. But it doesn't harm them permanently."

A naughty grin spread across Papa's face under his beard stubble. "I'll bet if you sprayed a bear with enough of Mimi's hair spray he'd be too stiff to run!" he said. "But his fur would look good!"

"Very funny!" Mimi said before her expression grew serious. "We do need to pick up some bear spray before we go into Yellowstone."

"Yes, you do," Owen said. "Bear attacks are rare. Bears normally try to avoid people, especially groups of people. But, you have to remember that grizzlies are huge, powerful, wild animals."

Brad looked at them with an **ominous** expression. "I hope you enjoyed my free demonstration," he said sourly. "Remember, encounters with bears can be deadly. It's best to mind your own business and steer clear of any business with grizzly bears."

10

PREDATOR PROGRAM

"Who wants to feed some bears?" Owen asked.

"Are you serious?" Evan replied. "Why feed something that can eat me?"

"I promise it's safe," Owen said. "The Keeper Kids is another one of the programs here to teach kids about bears."

"That sounds awesome," Avery said.

"Yeah!" Ella agreed. "Maybe I'll see my cub. And this time I've got my camera with me!"

"What cub?" Owen asked. They'd been so busy since arriving at the Grizzly & Wolf Discovery Center that Ella hadn't asked anyone about the cub.

"I didn't know a new cub had been brought in," Owen remarked. "That's usually big news around here."

"When Ella was lost in the forest," Evan explained, "she saw a bear cub wandering alone without its mother."

"Lost? It's a good thing they found you!" Owen said. "I guarantee you if you saw a bear cub, its mother was close by. A mama grizzly bear is one of the most protective animals of all."

They paused by the wolf enclosure to watch the young gray wolves frolicking in the tall grass. "If they weren't moving, I'm not sure I could see them in there," Ella said as she snapped a picture. Their coats, mottled shades of gray that ranged from almost white to charcoal, **camouflaged** them. When they dropped to their bellies, only their curious, candle-flame eyes were visible.

The wolves fascinated the two boys. Avery pulled Ella aside. "What do you think about Owen?" Avery asked. "He knew a lot about the bear break-ins in Cody, Wyoming.

Do you think they might be connected somehow to our cabin break-in?"

"I don't know," Ella said, confused. "But I think Brad acted super-strange, like he wanted us to get hurt by a bear. I don't think Brad likes Owen. I especially don't think Brad likes grizzly bears!"

"Hey," Owen said, "don't you want to see the wolves?" The girls ended their conversation and came closer to the wolf enclosure. Ella swung her camera around. Through the lens, she could see one of the wolves gnawing a bleached white bone. Ella patted the bone in her jacket pocket. *Had the bone she found been left over from something a wolf had killed? Had there been wolves in the forest that night, too, waiting to pounce on her and the cub?*

Ella just had to ask the question. "Do wolves hunt bears?" she asked Owen.

"They're both predators at the top of the food chain," Owen said. "But I doubt that one wolf could kill a fully-grown bear. That's not how wolves hunt anyway. They hunt in packs. A pack is a group of several wolves that live together. A pack might be able to hunt and kill a bear, especially a young bear cub or one that was sick or injured."

The wolf suddenly jumped to its feet, pointed its snout to the sky and let out a long howl. Ella tried to remember the ghostly howls in the forest from the night before. *This howl is different*, she thought.

"Why's he doing that?" Avery asked.

"Maybe he smells a pack of wild wolves in the distance," Owen said.

"Aren't they happy here?" Ella asked.

"They were brought here as young pups," Owen said. "This is the only home they can remember, so they probably couldn't live in the wild. But I'm glad that wild wolves have been reintroduced to Yellowstone."

"What do you mean reintroduced?" Avery asked. "I thought wolves have always lived in Yellowstone."

"They have," Owen said, "but the wolves were almost wiped out because of conflicts with humans. They sometimes killed the livestock of farmers and ranchers, so people wanted them gone."

"But I thought Yellowstone National Park was created to protect wildlife," Ella said.

"That's right! It was our first national park," Owen said. "In 1872, President Grant signed a law that made Yellowstone a national park and protected the area from being settled by people.

"But there was a problem," Owen continued. "People wanted to protect the natural wonders of Yellowstone like the geysers and ancient forests. But they didn't understand that the plant and animals living in Yellowstone were important too. Hunters were paid to kill the wolves. By the 1930s, all the wolves in Yellowstone were dead. Because there were so few wolves left in North America, wolves were placed on the **endangered species** list. Fortunately, there are now more than 300 wild wolves in Yellowstone. Wolf pups from other areas were raised here and put back into the wild—that's what I mean by 'reintroduced.'"

"Why did they decide to bring the wolves back to Yellowstone if everyone wanted them gone?" Ella asked.

"Scientists started noticing that strange things were happening," Owen explained. "Without wolves hunting the elk, there were too many elk. All those elk ate so many plants that there weren't enough plant roots to hold the soil in place. Without plant roots holding the soil, rainwater and river water began to **erode**, or wash away, the soil in Yellowstone. Some of the rivers even got wider because there was not enough brush along the banks."

"I get it!" Avery announced excitedly. "It's like a puzzle. Wolves are like a single piece of Yellowstone's puzzle. You need all parts—trees, bushes, wolves, elk, squirrels, and even bears—to complete the puzzle. Without the wolves, Yellowstone's **ecosystem** was out of balance."

"That's exactly right," Owen said. "Losing the wolves even hurt the bears. Because the elk ate so many berries, there weren't enough berries left for the bears. But now, the elk numbers are down."

"Because of the wolves?" Evan asked.

"Only partly," Owen said. "It's also because of the fish."

"What?!" Evan asked, imagining a fish attacking a big elk.

"One of the grizzlies' favorite foods is cutthroat trout," Owen explained.

"Do the bears cut their throats?" Evan said, rubbing his neck.

"No!" Owen said with a laugh. "They have a reddish pink mark under their bottom jaw that makes them look like their throat has been cut."

"Are those the fish you always see grizzlies catching in pictures?" Avery asked.

"Yes," Owen said. "When the cutthroat trout are swimming upstream to **spawn**, it's like an all-you-can-eat buffet for bears. But people have introduced a new species of trout into Yellowstone—the lake trout. Adult lake trout eat the young cutthroat trout before they can grow up. And the bears can't eat the lake trout because they don't come to the surface where the bears can catch them.

"To make matters worse," Owen continued, "drought and diseases have also harmed the bears' other favorite food— whitebark pine seed."

"So, the bears don't have as much food, and they're eating elk instead?" Avery asked.

"Exactly," Owen said, "and they're roaming farther outside Yellowstone to look for food, which causes more run-ins with people."

"Maybe that's why they were at our cabin," Evan suggested.

"It's almost like playing Jenga," Avery agreed. "If you take out one thing, everything else can crumble."

Owen nodded. "That's why my **ancestors** had so much respect for the wolves and bears. Every part of the Yellowstone environment is important, even the wild animals that can be scary to people."

Avery eyed Owen curiously. "Who were your ancestors?" she asked.

"The Shoshone Indians who once lived in Yellowstone before it was a national park," he replied. "That's why I want to become a wildlife biologist—so I can help protect wildlife, especially the grizzlies.

"Scientists believe that there were once as many as 50,000 grizzly bears in the lower 48 states," Owen added. "Like the wolves, they were once hunted almost to extinction. They were added to the endangered species list. Now there are only about 1,200 grizzlies living in the lower 48 states."

Evan saw Avery reaching for her phone, but stopped her. "I got this one," he said, marking the air with his finger.

"That's 48,800 fewer bears than there once was," he said. "And I figured it out without the use of technology!"

Owen lowered his voice and motioned for the three to get closer. "But you know," he whispered, "some people still don't like the grizzlies. Some people still hunt the grizzlies. These people are called poachers—people who hunt the grizzlies illegally. You three better be on the lookout for suspicious characters in Yellowstone. You wouldn't want to tangle with those folks."

11

HIDDEN MIDDEN

"This is Ranger Oakley," Owen said, introducing them to the supervisor of the bear feeding activity. "She's a Yellowstone park ranger who volunteers at the Center." Ranger Oakley wore her official ranger uniform, including a gray shirt and dark green pants. She was older than Owen or Brad, but still young and wore her hair in a ponytail pulled through the back of a baseball cap.

"Have you heard about a new cub that was brought here last night?" Ella blurted out. She was about to pop with eagerness for clues about the mysterious cub.

"No," Ranger Oakley answered. "I'm sure the Center managers would have told me."

"It's nice to meet you," Avery said

politely, giving Ella a "Have you forgotten your manners?" look.

Avery was feeling a bit too warm in her heavy jacket, so she took it off and hooked it on a branch of the tree they were standing near. "Do you know Ranger Warren?" she asked the ranger.

"I'm sorry, but I haven't met Ranger Warren yet," Ranger Oakley said. "I just started working in Yellowstone a few weeks ago."

Evan noticed the baseball cap Ranger Oakley wore with her uniform. "Where's your ranger hat?" he asked bluntly.

Ranger Oakley laughed as her face turned red. "It's a funny story," she said. "I stopped to lock down the lids on some garbage cans around a campsite. I left my hat in the truck. When I got back in my truck, my hat was gone! It's a mystery to me.

"Pretty embarrassing for a ranger though, huh?" Ranger Oakley continued. "I've ordered a new hat, but that hat was special. My daughter, Mary Beth, drew a big heart with her name inside it." She chuckled. "She said that she'd be on my mind everywhere I went."

As Owen promised, the bear habitat enclosure, which had fences twice as tall as Papa, was empty of bears. About a dozen excited kids waited to hide food for the bears to find. Ranger Oakley passed out fruits, seeds, nuts, and fish—all the bear favorites—to the children. They entered through a small gate and dashed around the bear's enclosure in search of places to hide the food.

"This looks like a great spot," Ella said, stashing a piece of apple and a handful of berries deep into the gap between two jagged gray rocks.

Evan wrinkled his nose at the trout he carried. He quickly found a small log with a hole in it and plopped the fish inside. "This is like an Easter egg hunt for bears," he said.

Avery was digging in a pile of leaves like an excited puppy. "Yep," she said, "except the bears would just eat the eggs, not put them in a basket!"

"No one can call them picky eaters," Ella agreed. "Just look at how many different kinds of food she gave us to hide!"

"That's why bears are called omnivores," Owen said. "Their mouths are designed to eat almost anything. They have sharp teeth for tearing meat like a carnivore, and flat teeth for grinding plants like an herbivore. Maybe that's why they get so big. Male bears can weigh close to 1,000 pounds!"

"There!" Avery said, patting the top of a mound of decaying leaves and dirt. She had a satisfied look on her face. "These leaves smell so moldy and musty there's no way a bear will pick up the scent of those white-bark pine seeds I hid under there."

"You made a midden," Owen said.

"You mean I made it hidden, don't you?" Avery asked.

"No," Owen replied. "You did the same thing the squirrels do in the forest. They gather the pine seeds and bury them in mounds called middens. The bears then come along and rob the middens."

"Ha ha!" Evan laughed. "I've always said you're squirrely!"

Avery wagged her finger at her little brother. "We'll just see who has the last laugh! If the bears find your food and Ella's before mine, the two of you will do my chores for a week."

"Deal!" Evan said.

"Now, wait a minute!" Ella whined. "What if we win?"

"Then you don't have to do my chores for a week!" Avery said.

Before Ella could protest the lopsided bet, Ranger Oakley said, "Time's up!"

The kids dashed for the gate. Ranger Oakley did a head count. "We're missing one," she said.

"It's Evan!" Avery cried. She looked through the wire fence to see Evan furiously kicking the log he hid the fish in, trying to roll it over.

"Evan!" Avery screamed at the top of her lungs.

"I'm just making sure no bear finds this fish!" he yelled.

Avery pointed at the other end of the enclosure where the bears would enter. "Bears are coming—hungry bears!"

When Evan realized he was the only one left in the enclosure, he thought for sure he was bear bait. He ran as fast as his short legs could carry him and slipped through the gate, breathless.

"You can't fool around when hungry bears are near," Ranger Oakley said. She quickly counted heads to make sure that every child was out, locked the enclosure gate, and called, "Let them out of the den!"

While the kids waited for the bears to enter the habitat, Avery saw Brad several yards away, talking to a man. Avery had noticed the man watching them while they hid the bear snacks. He appeared to take detailed notes and nodded often as Brad spoke. Brad was still wearing the bear costume, but the man was wearing jeans, a blue-and-black checked shirt, and brown hiking boots that looked just like the ones they'd bought for Papa.

"Do you know that man?" Avery asked Owen.

"I've never seen him before," Owen answered. "Why?"

Avery wrinkled her nose. "It's just that he's wearing the same type of boots that went missing from our cabin."

"That's not enough evidence to accuse someone of a crime," Owen said, chuckling. "Everybody around here owns a pair of those hiking boots."

"Oh!" Ella exclaimed. "Here come the bears! I think I'll be the winner," she bragged. "There's no way a bear can smell through solid rock."

"Maybe, maybe not," Owen replied. "But I have to warn you that bears have an extremely good sense of smell—even better than a hound dog! There's an old Native American saying about the animals' senses. It goes, 'A pine needle fell in the forest. The eagle saw it, the deer heard it, and the bear smelled it.'"

One by one, the bears lumbered into the enclosure. An old bear with chestnut fur and a white muzzle ambled toward the pile of leaves. Ella watched every move he made.

"I'll bet he finds Avery's first," she said. But to her surprise, he walked right past the leaves.

With his nose sucking in scents like a vacuum cleaner, he went right to the crevice where Ella buried the berries. "Oh, no!" she cried as the animal casually pushed back the stone with his massive claws and began munching. The old bear looked straight at Ella with a bored expression that seemed to say, 'Too easy!' and moved on in search of more snacks.

A younger, tan-colored bear rolled Evan's log over and quickly speared the fish with claws as long as human fingers. He held it up like it was prime rib on a fork and chomped off its head in one smack.

"I guess you could say that fish came to a **grisly** end," Avery said.

"Everything a grizzly eats comes to a grisly end," Evan said. "How do you think they got their name?"

"It has nothing to do with the way they eat," Avery said smugly. "They got their name because their fur has little white tips on the end. That's what you call grizzled."

"I still like my explanation better," Evan said.

"Look!" Owen said. "The old sow is headed for Avery's leaf pile!"

"What sow?" Ella asked. She had visited enough farms to know that female pigs are called sows. "Are there pigs in there with the bears?"

Owen shook his head. "Female bears are called sows, just like female pigs are called sows."

"Then the male bears are called boars?" Ella asked.

"That's right," Owen said.

The sow tore into Avery's leaf pile and quickly devoured the seeds inside. "Oh well," Avery said. "I guess our hiding skills are no match for a bear's nose, but at least my hiding place was the last one found. I'll give each of you your chore list as soon as we get home!"

Ella sighed. "Don't be so sad," Avery said. "It's only for a week."

"It's not the chores," Ella said. "All the bears came out, but my bear cub wasn't with them. Ranger Warren said if he was found, he'd be brought here, but no one has seen him. What could have happened to him?"

But different questions haunted Avery's mind. *If bears are omnivores that will eat almost anything, then why was the food in the cabin strewn, but not eaten? Had whatever made those oval footprints scared the bears away?*

When they were ready to go, Avery went to grab her jacket off the tree. She was shocked to see that one of the arms was torn—like a bear took a bite out of it. "What in the world?" she asked no one in particular. As she examined the tear, she heard the sound of crinkling paper in one of the pockets. She pulled the paper out and read:

Mind your own business and don't get clever when there are plenty of bear teeth around!

A grizzly bear catches a fish.

12

GIANT TEDDY

Avery had already told Ella and Evan about the card she found near the cabin. She didn't know what the words on it meant. Now, there was no hiding the ripped jacket and the meaning of the note.

When Owen asked about her sleeve, Avery claimed the tree did it. But later, she whispered to Ella, "Someone thinks we're on to them. I think they want us out of Yellowstone!"

"But who and why?" Ella asked.

"Well, I don't think a bear wrote that note!" Avery said. "But we need to be careful—very careful!"

When Owen suggested a visit to the museum at the Discovery Center, Avery checked the time on her phone. "We're supposed to meet Mimi and Papa at the gate soon," she said.

"It won't take long," Owen said, leading them to a building. "There, you can see the bears up close and personal."

"We haven't seen all the bears yet?" Ella asked. She was hopeful that she still might find her bear cub at the Center.

When they entered the museum, they were shocked to see an 8-foot-tall teddy bear! And snuggled in its arms were Mimi and Papa!

"How do you like our giant bear sofa?" Owen asked.

"Well, it looked so comfy we just couldn't *bear* passing by without having a sit!" Mimi said.

Evan picked up Mimi's pun and ran with it. "Seeing the two of you on that sofa is more than I can *bear*!" he added.

"My turn," Avery said. "I can't *bear* to see that picture of Evan on the *bear*-skin rug when he was a baby. He was totally *bare*!"

"OK! You win the pun-off," Evan said, turning redder than a Montana sunset.

"Mimi and I already went through the museum," Papa said. "You kids go ahead. We'll wait here. I can't *bear* to leave this sofa!"

As Avery turned to leave, Mimi noticed her coat. "What on earth happened to your coat?" she asked. Not wanting to worry her grandmother, Avery muttered something about the tree snagging it and quickly chased after Evan and Ella.

The museum was far from what Ella hoped for. There were plenty of bears—some were even cubs—but none of them were alive. They were mounted and stuffed, just like the giant teddy bear sofa. Her hopes dropped like a rock down the side of a mountain.

"Hey, look at this!" Evan said, running for a glass counter display. "More bear scat. And, wow, this one ate a lot of seeds!"

"That's another good thing that bears do," Owen said. "They leave behind seed that can grow, along with ready-made fertilizer!"

Avery found a large map of Yellowstone that showed the different wildlife habitats in the park. The Alpine tundra habitat near the mountaintops had pictures of mountain goats and tiny mammals called pika that looked like a cross between a rabbit and a rat. The mountain meadow habitat included pictures of pronghorn, elk, and mule deer, while the sage-steppe grasslands habitat included beautiful wildflowers and bison. Avery knew the great grizzly bear felt at home in the habitats of Yellowstone.

As Avery made her way down the long map case, she saw that Brad stepped in beside her to clean the glass case. "Always fingerprints!" he huffed.

"Hello, Brad!" Avery said. "I really enjoyed your demonstration with the bearskin this morning!"

"Yeah, right," Brad said. "I've got work to do, kid."

Avery blushed. "You don't have to be so rude," she muttered.

"You'd be rude too if you had to talk to all the strange people I have to," Brad said mysteriously.

Ella suddenly called from the other side of the museum. "Avery! You need to see this!"

Standing between the skeleton of an adult bear and a much smaller one, Ella had a sad look on her face. "Awwww!" she cried. "This was probably a mama bear and her cub about the same age as the cub I saw."

"Do you still have the bone with you?" Avery asked.

"Sure," Ella said. "It's right here."

Ella took the scarf-wrapped bone out of her pocket. Avery compared the bones to the bones of the skeleton. When she reached the foot, she exclaimed, "That's it—a perfect match! The bone you found came from a bear's foot—a baby bear's foot!"

Before Ella could respond, a red-faced Owen yelled from across the room, "What do you think you're doing?!"

13

DEAD RINGER

Owen charged toward them, his long black hair bouncing. "I can't believe you'd mess with a display like that," he said, snatching the bone from Avery. "You're not supposed to touch these!"

"But, but, I, d-d-didn't," Avery stammered, shocked at Owen's outburst.

"Oh yeah?" he said **sarcastically**. "Then where did you get this? You plucked it from the skeleton display, right?"

"I found it in the forest!" Ella exclaimed. She told Owen everything that happened since they came to Yellowstone. It was hard to believe so many things had happened in only two days. Owen studied Ella's face and then looked at the bear skeleton. Nothing seemed out of place. "I believe you," he said, "and I'm sorry I freaked out. If I got in trouble because of you, I wouldn't be able to volunteer here anymore."

"What do you think about the bone?" Avery asked.

Owen compared it to the skeleton just as Avery had done. "A **dead ringer**," he said, studying it carefully.

Ella read the plaque beside the skeleton. "It says that bears walk the same way people walk—with the heel and sole flat on the ground. There's a big word for it—**plantigrade**."

Avery looked at the picture of bear prints on the plaque and counted the five toes. *That's the same animal footprint I saw behind the cabin. Maybe it really was a bear stomping around our cabin after all! But wait— that doesn't explain those other strange oval marks. Who could those they belong to?*

Owen pointed to a ring of triangular scratches on the bone from the forest. "Did any of you notice these marks?"

Ella gulped. "No," she said. "Are those tooth marks?"

"They're tooth marks, all right," Owen said. "But not the kind you're thinking of. These marks were made by the teeth of a steel trap."

Ella buried her face in her hands. "That poor little bear!" she wailed.

On their way back to meet Mimi and Papa, the kids passed by the habitat map again. Avery noticed an odd sticker stuck on the corner that she hadn't noticed before. It was a square made up of smaller black and white squares.

"Stop!" she said, pulling out her phone. "That looks like a QR code." She had learned in her technology class that QR, or Quick Response Codes, could be scanned for additional information. She held her phone steady as the red line of her QR scanner moved across the square.

"That's funny," Avery said. "These things usually give you a website address to visit, but this one is weird." She held it up for the other kids to see:

WHERE THE
DRAGON
SLEEPS.
WE'LL BE
AFTER THE
SLEUTH.

Avery's mind was racing. None of it made any sense! *After the sleuth? A sleuth is someone who wants to solve a mystery. Could I be the sleuth they're after?*

14

EXPLODING PIE

The kids found Mimi and Papa still sitting on the teddy bear sofa. Papa, loyal to his habit of reading a newspaper each day, was finally reading the one he bought that morning. Evan snuck up and thumped the paper to get his attention. Papa slowly lowered the paper and bared his teeth in a growl. "Don't you know better than to bother a grouchy old grizzly when he's reading the paper?" he said. His growl quickly changed to a grin. "You kids ready to go?"

"Yes," Ella said, "if you can wake Mimi."

Papa hadn't noticed that Mimi had become so relaxed on the big bear sofa that she had flopped over on the arm and fallen asleep. Papa nudged her. Mimi stretched.

"Is it spring already?" she said with a big, bright smile.

"Far from it," Papa said. "The paper said we should expect freezing temperatures tonight, maybe even a few snowflakes! Perfect weather for camping in Yellowstone!"

"Brrrr!" Mimi said, pulling on her jacket. "Don't you think it's too cold to camp tonight?" she asked hopefully. "Maybe we should stay in a motel room."

"You're here for inspiration, not comfort!" Papa reminded her. "That's why I want to take you to Inspiration Point. It's near Canyon Campground where I reserved our campsite." He tapped her head. "Nothin' like crisp wilderness air to get those imagination wheels turning."

"Or wheels frozen," Mimi mumbled.

"Besides, Mimi," Avery said, "you know you'll be sleeping on top of a volcano! What's warmer than that?"

"What are you talking about, Avery?" Evan asked.

"We learned all about it in science this year," Avery explained. "Yellowstone National

Park sits on top of a super volcano called the Yellowstone Caldera."

"What's a caldera?" Evan asked.

"A caldera is like a volcano, but it doesn't look like a mountain," Avery explained. "A caldera is more bowl-shaped and is sunken into the ground. My teacher said it's like the crust of a pie. But instead of cherry filling, there's magma underneath."

"Magma is melted rock!" Evan said proudly.

"That's right," Avery said. "And the heat from magma deep under the Earth's crust is what causes all the **geothermal** features of Yellowstone."

"The G-O-what?" Evan asked.

"You know, the bubbling, steamy stuff under Yellowstone, like Old Faithful," Avery explained. "It's kind of like the steam coming out of the slits in the pie crust!"

"That would be one big pie!" Owen said. "The Yellowstone Caldera is around 45 miles long and 34 miles wide!"

"To find area, multiply length times width," Avery mumbled, while using her calculator app. "Wow!" she exclaimed. "That's 1,530 square miles!"

"That would be enough pie to last me a lifetime!" Evan exclaimed.

"The problem is some scientists believe Yellowstone has exploded twice in the last 2 million years. They think it might explode again in the future," Owen said. "They just don't know when!"

"Why would the pie explode?" Evan asked.

"When too much heat, magma, and gas build up under the crust," Owen explained, "it finally goes POP!" Owen made an exploding gesture with his hands.

Evan's eyes grew wide. "Guess I better not jump around," he said. "I don't want to poke a hole in the crust and cause an eruption!"

Evan's statement tickled Papa. As he laughed, the newspaper slid off his lap and hit the floor with a dull crinkle. Avery picked it up, and a headline snagged her eye:

WEST YELLOWSTONE NEWS

Two Cody Cabins Ransacked, Authorities Suspect Bear

Avery glanced at Owen, who was still laughing at Evan. *Hadn't he asked Papa if they were staying in Cody when he learned that their cabin was ransacked? Had he read the paper that morning, or did he have inside information? Owen could have easily slipped the note into her jacket when she wasn't looking. And the way he reacted about the bone Ella had found—did Owen have something to hide?* Avery decided it was best to keep an eye on Owen.

Avery had an idea. "Hey," she said. "What we really need for our camping trip is a Yellowstone guide!"

The others looked at her curiously. Avery smiled at Owen. "Do you think your parents would let you go with us?"

"It's an awesome idea!" Evan said. "Then I wouldn't be the only boy with all these girls!"

As Mimi spoke with Owen's parents to explain their plans, Avery ripped out the newspaper article before dropping the rest of the paper into a nearby recycling bin.

There's no way the same bear that busted up our cabin ran all the way across Yellowstone National Park and did it to another cabin during the same night, she thought. *There's something more afoot here than hungry bears!*

15

BUFFALO BY ANY OTHER NAME

"Are we there yet?" Evan asked. He was squished in the back seat of Papa's truck like a fat bear in a tiny den.

Avery, relieved that Owen got permission to go camping with them asked, "Are you kidding? We just pulled out of Owen's driveway!" They had stopped by Owen's house to pick up supplies he said he needed.

"I know," Evan said, "but it's my job to ask that!"

Avery charted the route to Canyon Campground with the map app on her phone.

Ten minutes later, Papa took a right turn. "You took a wrong turn, Papa!" Avery warned. "This isn't the way to Canyon Campground."

"Do you think I'd bring you to Yellowstone National Park without a visit to Old Faithful?" he asked.

Avery saw Mimi smiling into the rearview mirror. "Papa always manages a few fun **detours** along the way," she said. "He's our 'Old Faithful.'"

Ella whispered to Avery, "Have you figured out the QR code message?"

Avery looked at Owen to gauge his reaction. "I don't know where the dragon sleeps," she said. "But someone knows we're sleuths, and they're after us."

Owen looked puzzled. "I thought you said the message was about bears," he said.

"What do mystery-solving sleuths have to do with bears?" Ella asked.

"Oh!" Owen exclaimed. "I get it. You thought 'sleuth' meant detective. But the word 'sleuth' is also the name for a group of bears."

Being careful to keep her voice down, Ella whispered, "Really? So no one's after us?" Ella began to understand the message better.

Avery added, "So, if they're not after us, then they're after the bears!"

"Wait!" said Owen. "All this time you were thinking someone was after you? You guys are acting like you're trying to solve some kind of mystery or something."

The siblings looked at each other and then back at Owen.

"Really?" he asked. "Wow!"

"Owen, I'm worried. This QR code message sounds an awful lot like someone is going to harm the bears!" cried Avery.

EEEERRRRKKKKKK!!!!! Papa slammed on the brakes. The kids lurched forward. Dust swirled around a thundering rumble in front of the truck.

"Wild bison!" Mimi exclaimed. "They look like they're wearing wooly shawls across their shoulders!"

"Whew!" Papa said, wiping his pale face with his hand. "I wonder what has them stirred up?"

"This is better than any wildlife movie!" Evan exclaimed. "I didn't know they had bison and buffalo in Yellowstone!"

"What people in the United States call buffalo are really bison," Owen explained. "The only true buffalo are in Africa and Asia."

"You mean like water buffalo? Ella asked.

"Yep," Owen said. "Bison have a hump on their shoulders and buffalo don't. Just like grizzly bears have a hump on their shoulders and black bears don't. That's how you can tell them apart from a distance."

Something moved in Evan's **peripheral** vision. He spun his head toward the passenger side window. "Whatever you call them, there's one ch-ch-ch-charging right at us!"

16

GEYSER GUESTS

"Floor it, Papa!" Ella yelled.

The truck leaped ahead. The kids about-faced to watch the herd of bison bolt across the road behind them.

Mimi held her heart. "That bison needs glasses!" she said.

With no more close encounters of the wildlife kind, Papa soon pulled into the Old Faithful Visitor Center. Inside, a gigantic window with a spectacular view of the famous geyser welcomed them.

"I'm not impressed," Evan said sadly as he watched Old Faithful. "I thought it would be bigger."

"It's not erupting right now," Mimi explained.

Avery noticed a ring of white around the geyser's round hole. "That's not snow, is it?" she asked Mimi.

"No," Mimi said. "That's called sinter. When the geyser erupts, it carries minerals from underground and deposits them on the surface. Those minerals form a special white deposit called sinter."

"The white sinter reminds me of a donut covered in powdered sugar," Avery said.

Evan and Ella headed for the young scientist section of the Visitor Center. Avery made a beeline to a glass-enclosed display to read about minerals that form sinter. A man's reflection in the glass distracted her. Dressed in a cap with flaps over the ears and a heavy plaid jacket, the man studied a detailed map of the area. There was nothing too unusual about him until he looked up. Avery recognized his face immediately. "Ranger Warren?" she asked.

She saw the man's reflected eyes look directly at her, but instead of answering, he quickly slipped through the crowd and toward the door.

Avery plowed through the visitors to follow him, hoping to ask him some questions, but a group of kindergartners blocked her way. When she finally reached the door, Ranger Warren was gone.

"Old Faithful is expected to erupt in just a few minutes," the Visitor Center's loudspeaker announced. "Please take your seats."

Avery spotted Mimi herding their group toward the door. "Let's hurry so we can get a good viewing spot," Mimi said.

Outside, the kids scrambled to the top of a metal viewing stand, while Mimi and Papa took a seat at the bottom.

"Some engineer needs to design something that would take all that steam from Old Faithful and warm these cold metal seats," suggested Evan. "My bottom is freezing!"

"Metal is a good conductor," Avery said, shaking her head. "It does a good job of carrying the heat away from your bottom which leaves it feeling cold."

"Stop conducting my heat!" Evan scolded the metal seat.

Avery giggled at her brother and then motioned for them all to huddle around her. "I saw Ranger Warren," she said. "He wasn't wearing his uniform. Why would he be in the park if he was not on duty?"

"Maybe he's working undercover," Owen suggested. "Maybe he's headed to Cody to investigate those other ransacked cabins."

Avery eyed Owen suspiciously. "How did you know about those cabins?" she asked.

"Brad told me," he said. "I guess he heard it on the news or something."

Avery remembered Brad's rude behavior and wondered if he knew more than he could have learned from a news report.

"I made an important discovery in the Visitor Center," Ella announced. "I learned that there is a geothermal feature in Yellowstone called the Dragon's Mouth. Didn't the last clue say something about a dragon?"

"Yes, it—"Avery began to say.

"Whoa!" interrupted Evan when the ground beneath rumbled. "That sounded like one of my burps after eating Mimi's spaghetti!"

The steamy water of Old Faithful barely surfaced from the ground, but it rose higher with each new blurp until it finally exploded into a 130-foot column that tickled the pink-tinged sky like a feather.

"I feel the mist on my face!" Evan said, sticking out his tongue. "I want to tell everyone back home that I drank from Old Faithful."

As Old Faithful shrank back to the ground, Avery combed the tourists with her eyes, hoping to spot Ranger Warren. All she saw was a green pickup truck speeding away from the parking lot.

Old Faithful

17

BEAR ALARM

The sun was sinking below the tree-lined horizon when they got back on the road. Papa watched carefully for more wildlife surprises.

When they found their campsite it was pitch dark, save for the icy stars that winked above. As they set up their tent, Mimi rustled up some camp stew on the grill.

"I can't eat another bite," Evan said, tossing a piece of bread on the ground.

"Unless you want furry visitors tonight, don't do that," Owen warned, rushing to pick it up and drop it in the trash bag. When they finished eating, he made sure the trash bag went into the campground's bear-proof garbage container and that the cooking pot was thoroughly cleaned.

"I knew it was a good idea to bring a bear expert along," Avery said and smiled at Owen.

But Owen was still busy inspecting the campsite. "Mimi," he said. "Don't go to sleep in those clothes you cooked in. A bear might think you smell like leftovers!"

"Thanks, Owen," she said. "We'll put them in the food locker and tie it all up in the tree."

"I just noticed," Ella said, "that the trees in the campground are the same kind of trees I saw when I was lost in the forest."

"These are lodgepole pines," Owen said. "My ancestors used them for the poles of their lodges, or teepees."

When Mimi and Papa crawled into the tent to listen to the news on their battery-powered radio, Avery, Ella, and Owen lay on the dry grass with their hands behind their heads and stared at the sky. Evan leaned against a tree and played with some sticks and twine.

"Oh, look," Avery exclaimed. "I can see the Great Bear and the Little Bear constellations!"

"Are you interested in astronomy?" Owen asked.

"I'm mostly interested in bears right now," Avery answered. "If someone planned to get bears to go where they wanted them to go, how would they do it?"

"By promising them a treat?" Ella suggested.

"That's exactly what I was thinking," Avery said, remembering the man in the hiking boots taking notes at the bear habitat enclosure at the Grizzly & Wolf Discovery Center.

A sudden tinkling sound interrupted their conversation. "What is that?" Ella asked.

"I engineered a bear alarm system!" Evan announced. "Those rascals will never get past this to wreck our tent! Will you help me set it up?"

Evan had gathered a bundle of twigs from the forest. Together, the kids tapped the twigs into the ground in a circle around the campsite. Evan followed them, tying twine to each one until it made a complete circle. Then, he attached bells to the twine.

"Where'd you get those bells?" Ella asked.

"Remember that wind chime Mimi bought?" he asked. "It's not gonna chime until it's put back together."

"If a bear tries to get into our tent, it will hit the twine and make the bells ring!" Ella said. "This is **ingenious**, Evan!" *I just hope we don't need it*, she thought.

"Do you remember what Ella said about the Dragon's Mouth?" Avery asked.

"Yeah," Owen said. "It's a geological feature like a small cave. Hot spring water from underneath the Earth's surface boils up through the cave. The steam coming from the hot water looks like smoke blowing out of a dragon's mouth."

"Ooooh," Evan said, his eyes getting wider. "I think I understand the message now. Do you think someone is trying to catch the bears near the Dragon's Mouth?"

"I can't figure out *why* someone would try to catch my bear cub," Ella remarked.

"We'll have to investigate the dragon's mouth in the morning," Avery said.

As the night went on, Mimi and Papa fell asleep. Owen entertained Avery, Evan, and Ella with stories about Yellowstone and the Shoshone Indians. After a while, everyone fell asleep except Avery. She still didn't quite trust Owen. She had hidden one of the bells in her pocket when building the bear alarm. She took the bell from her pocket and crawled to the tent door where Owen had left his boots. She quietly tied the bell to Owen's bootlaces.

That way, he can't do anything sneaky without me knowing, she thought.

18

DRAGON BREATH

Avery sat up. Was that a bell tinkling? She fumbled for her phone's flashlight app, unzipped her sleeping bag, and crawled to the flap to look outside. A thin smear of snow sparkled in the dawn's early light. Relieved that she didn't see a bear, she woke the other kids, being careful not to wake Mimi and Papa in the process.

"We've had company!" she whispered. The kids followed her outside. Stamped in the snow were bear prints and the strange ovals that were in the woods and at the cabin. The bear prints stopped around the tent, but the ovals led off into the trees.

Owen shook his foot, the bell tinkling. "Hey, what is this?" he asked. Avery looked down at her feet to avoid looking at Owen. *Better safe than sorry,* she thought.

"It must have gotten tangled up in your boots last night," Evan said as Owen bent down and untied the bell.

"It's time to get to the bottom of this," Avery said. She plugged the Dragon's Mouth into her phone's GPS and waited for walking directions. The kids, who had slept in their clothes, quickly pulled on their boots, hoping they could investigate before Mimi and Papa awoke.

"Wait!" Owen said, running back to the tent for his bear spray. They followed the oval prints along a dirt path through the woods. After a very long hike, the strange ovals disappeared as the path turned into a boardwalk leading to the mouth of a cave.

"That must be the Dragon's Mouth!" Ella said, pointing to a small cave belching steam. Even though it was freezing, a small pool of water bubbled hot at the cave's mouth.

"Uhhgg," Evan said, fanning his nose. "That dragon must've eaten rotten eggs for lunch. His breath stinks! Now I know what people mean when they say dragon breath!"

"That's hydrogen sulfide gas that comes out of the ground here," Owen said.

A deafening roar suddenly cracked through the crisp air.

"Grizzlies!" Avery said, pointing into the distance. Above them on a hillside, they could see massive dark bear-shapes moving through the morning fog. Some were hunched over something on the ground and growling.

"They're fighting over food!" Owen said.

"Weren't you nosy kids warned to stay away?" a voice suddenly echoed from behind them.

When the kids pivoted to find the voice, they spotted a man standing alone in the small parking lot. Avery recognized him as the man who had been watching the grizzly feeding and taking notes. *I think that's the same guy I saw Brad talking to—the guy with the brown boots like Papa's,* she thought.

"They like trout the most!" he said to Owen. "Your friend at the Discovery Center was kind enough to give me all the information I needed to bait these bears."

"You mean Brad told you how to bait the bears?" Owen cried.

"The poor guy was just doing his job," the man said, shrugging his shoulders.

"We better get out of here," Avery said. But the man had now moved to block their retreat from the Dragon's Mouth. They were stuck between grizzly bears and a tough situation. Thinking quickly, Avery shrunk back behind Owen and pulled out her cell phone. She texted Mimi and Papa, telling them to call the Yellowstone Park Rangers to come to Dragon's Mouth. She just hoped the rangers would get there in time!

"What are you going to do with the bears?" Evan asked.

"Bears are very valuable, you know," the man said. "Those rangers have been after us for weeks. And you kids are threatening to ruin it for us."

The man came closer, walking slowly. "Now the question is, what should I do with you?" he said.

"Let us go!" cried Ella, trying to hold back tears.

"I can't do that," he said, "now you know we've been trapping bears. I think you might make a tasty snack for a hungry grizzly."

Just then, a green ranger truck whipped into the parking lot. They watched Ranger Warren, still out of uniform, climb out.

"You kids shouldn't be here," Ranger Warren said. "You better come with me."

"Thank goodness you're here!" Ella said. "This is the second time you've rescued me!"

"Come on, kids," Ranger Warren coaxed. "Those bears are angry!" Avery, Ella, Evan, and Owen sprinted past the man, who let them escape now that the Ranger Warren arrived.

"Ranger Warren," Owen said anxiously, "do you know what that man is trying to do? You need to arrest him."

"Yes, I do," Ranger Warren replied. "We've been trying to hunt him down for some time now." He turned to the man. "You stay right here, and I'll deal with you in a minute." Avery thought it strange that Ranger Warren said this with a slight smile, almost a smirk.

She also thought it strange that the man didn't try to run or escape.

When Ranger Warren opened his truck door to let them inside, Avery noticed that the familiar park service arrowhead emblem was suspiciously crooked. "A magnet," she said, ripping it away. The sign underneath said "Wildlife Removal." "So *that* was the card I found near the cabin," she said, putting the clues together. "And you had left a message for that other man to get bait—bait to trap the bears!"

She slipped her phone to Owen and mouthed, "Call for help!"

"You're no ranger!" Avery yelled to distract Warren's attention, as Owen crept to the other side of the truck and crouched beside a wheel. "You're a fake!"

"Well, those bears aren't fake!" Ranger Warren said, pointing to the growling bears. "You'd better get in this truck if you know what's good for you!"

Avery saw a ranger hat lying on the seat. "That's not really your hat, is it?" she said, grabbing it.

Avery flipped the hat over and saw the heart Ranger Oakley had described. It was signed, Mary Beth. "You stole it from Ranger Oakley!" she cried.

Owen handed Avery her cell phone and whispered, "Wait just a minute more!"

"Avery," Ella said nervously, pointing at the other man storming their way.

"I'll take care of these kids!" he threatened.

"I'm not scared of you, boot thief," Avery said. "I know you stole those boots when you wrecked our cabin!" The two men were closing in on Avery. She slipped between them, and the two men chased after her toward the parking lot.

Suddenly, a park ranger truck whipped into the parking lot, its yellow lights flashing and tires screeching. Two more park service vehicles followed and surrounded them. Ranger Oakley stepped out of the truck.

"You're under arrest," she told Warren, slapping handcuffs on his wrists. The other man ran toward a grove of trees.

"You know those grizzlies will hunt you down. You won't last long in the cold and the wild all by yourself," Ranger Oakley yelled after him. The man stopped, raised his hands in the air, and returned for the cuffs.

"I guess I'd rather face the law than a wild grizzly, too," Evan said.

Ranger Oakley put the men in one of the other vehicles. "I suggest we go someplace to talk before those bears finish their fish," she said.

"I know just the place," Avery said.

19

NOT ROGUE AT ALL

"Thanks for getting my hat back," Ranger Oakley told Avery as they drove to the place where Ella was found in the forest. After they had explained things to Mimi and Papa, Papa agreed to help Ranger Oakley find the spot. Ella told him her story of the cub and the strange noises. She suspected there was something more to find there.

"With his ranger uniform and fake truck, Warren drove around in Yellowstone without attracting attention," Ranger Oakley said. "But how did you know he was a fake?"

"I thought something about him was fishy when he came to the cabin," she explained. "He mentioned scratches on the refrigerator that he hadn't even seen yet!"

"We found a board with nails in the back of Warren's truck," Ranger Oakley said. "The nails were spaced like bear teeth. They probably used that board to make the scratches on your refrigerator."

"But what about the bear prints around the cabin?" Ella asked.

"That's easy," Avery said. "They made casts of real bear prints to stamp on the ground, but they were too lazy to make them look like a bear walking."

"You mean they made a whole bear paw out of plaster?" Ella asked.

"Yep," Avery said. "That wasn't donut powder on Warren's pants—it was plaster dust! I'm still not sure about those strange oval footprints, though," she added.

"They wore booties like doctors wear in the hospital," Ranger Oakley said. "We found the booties in the truck too. They were trying to hide their footprints."

"Why were they doing all this?" Evan asked.

"To make the bears look bad," Avery said.

"That's right," Ranger Oakley said. "We've wondered why there's been so many 'rogue' bears lately. Thanks to you, we now know these rogue bears aren't rogue at all. This gang wanted to keep real rangers busy investigating rogue bears while they killed innocent bears they baited with food. If caught, they could claim they killed a problem bear that broke into a cabin."

"I guess they were trying to get as many bears as possible before the bears went into hibernation for the winter," Owen said. "It's hard to find them then."

"Yes," Ranger Oakley said. "They tried to lure as many bears as possible out of Yellowstone. But with time running out, they started baiting them inside the park."

"But why did they want to kill bears?" Ella asked, still thinking about the little cub.

"Bear parts are valuable to people who trade illegal things, like bearskins," Ranger Oakley said. "Bear **gall bladders** are worth a lot of money. People in some parts of the world think they have amazing healing properties, and they'll pay a high price for them."

"This place looks familiar," Ella said as they drove through lodgepole pines. Ranger Oakley pulled off the road and Papa pulled in behind her. They followed Ella into a small clearing. White bones shone bright in the early morning sun.

"There's the tree with the twisted knot!" Avery said. "The one in the picture!"

"Looks like they've been at this for a while," Ranger Oakley said, shaking her head sadly. "This grizzly graveyard of bones will help lock up those men for a long time."

The same mournful sound that Ella heard at night drifted toward them. Ranger Oakley followed the sound to a pit dug in the ground. He motioned for them to come closer.

When they peered into the deep pit, the sad eyes of a mama grizzly met theirs. "This was one way they were trapping bears," Ranger Oakley said. "If Ella hadn't accidentally interrupted their plans that night when she got lost, this mama bear would already be dead."

"Look!" Ella exclaimed joyfully. Peeking from behind a tree was a small bear cub. "That's him! I told you I wasn't making it up!"

20

BEAR CLAWS AND BARE FEET

The Yellowstone Rangers tranquilized the mama bear to keep her calm and pulled her from the pit. Ranger Oakley invited Mimi, Papa, the kids and Jewel the dog to assist with a 'hard release.' This is a strategy to make bears extremely afraid of coming near humans.

They watched from the bed of the truck as the mama bear slowly gained consciousness. Ranger Oakley held Jewel's collar tightly as the mama bear struggled to stand on wobbly legs.

The mama bear sniffed the ground and looked curiously at them. Ella gripped her garbage can lids like cymbals. Evan held the bells from Mimi's wind chime. Owen had a drumstick poised above a traditional Shoshone drum. Mimi clutched her camp cooking pot and a big metal spoon. Papa was ready to clap his ham-sized hands together.

Avery found their noise-making methods old-fashioned. She downloaded an app that sounded like a stadium full of screaming football fans.

"I feel so mean scaring them this way!" Ella said.

"It may seem cruel," Ranger Oakley said, "but if they're afraid of humans, we'll never have to worry about them getting into trouble with humans again. They can live out their lives in this great park, wild and free, the way grizzlies are supposed to."

"She's coming to her senses," he warned. "On the count of three. ONE... TWO...THREE!!!"

Ranger Oakley released Jewel, who bounded toward the mama bear and her cub, barking ferociously. Everyone made noise. "Yah! Get out of here, bears! Don't come back! Be free! Stay away!" They whooped and hollered until the bears, with Jewel in hot pursuit, disappeared into the wilderness.

When Jewel jogged back to the truck, she wagged her tail happily.

"Have a happy life, little friend," Ella said, blowing a kiss into the wind.

"Thanks to you, that'll probably be about 30 years," Owen said.

"It's time to set one more bear free," Mimi told Papa. She pulled a shaving razor from her bag. "Come here, you old grizzly."

"OK!" said Papa, stroking his stubbly beard. "I promise I'll shave it off soon. But could this old bear buy everyone a round of bear claws at the donut shop first?"

"Deal!" they all cried.

"Wait," Ranger Oakley said, opening her truck to pull out a pair of hiking boots. "I need to return this stolen property to you. That man admitted he took them from your cabin."

Papa turned up his nose. "No thanks," he said. "I don't want to wear them after that scoundrel had them on his feet. He probably stepped in a lot of scat. I would rather have 'bare' feet, pardon the pun!"

Evan giggled. "Yes, Papa," he said, "if you wore those boots, Mimi would definitely tell you to scat!"

"I'm so sorry you all got wrapped up in this mess," Ranger Oakley said. "Yellowstone National Park is about sharing the beauty of nature and making great family memories."

"Yes, I think we've made a few memories to add to our travel log," Mimi said, with a twinkle in her eye. "And I think I've found all the inspiration I was looking for. Mission accomplished, sleuths!"

The End

DO YOU LIKE MYSTERIES?

You have the chance to solve them!
You can solve little mysteries,
like figuring out
how to do your homework and
why your dog always hides your shoes.

You can solve big mysteries, like how to
program a fun computer game,
protect an endangered animal,
find a new energy source,
INVENT A NEW WAY TO DO SOMETHING, explore
outer space, and more!

You may be surprised to find
that *science*, **technology**,
engineering, math, and even
HISTORY, literature, and
ART can help you solve all kinds of
"mysteries" you encounter.

So feed your curiosity, learn all you can, apply
your creativity, and **be a mystery-solver too!**

— Carole Marsh

More about the Science, Technology,
Engineering, & Math in this book ➜

GRIZZLY FACTS

- Grizzly bears are great swimmers and even better runners—grizzly bears can run across land at about 35 miles per hour. That's about as fast as a horse!

- Grizzly bears eat a LOT! When preparing for winter hibernation, grizzlies can eat up to 90 pounds of food a day!

- Unlike many animals, bears see in color, just like we do.

- Talk about terrific sniffers—grizzly bears can smell food from miles away!

- Bears are hunters, but they are also grazers. Approximately 75% of what grizzly bears eat is grass, berries, roots, and other plants. The other 25% is fish, deer, elk, rodents, honey, and even insects.

- Standing upright, a grizzly can be more than 8 feet tall!

- Some grizzlies grow to weigh more than 800 pounds!

- Biologists estimate 50,000 grizzlies once lived in the United States. Today, there are only between 1,200 and 1,400 grizzlies in the United States. It is important to protect and respect these rare, wild animals.

- Grizzly bear mothers often give birth to cubs during hibernation.

- Grizzly attacks on humans are very rare, but that does not mean grizzlies are cuddly teddy bears. Grizzlies are unpredictable wild animals and are best left undisturbed.

WHEN IN BEAR COUNTRY

NEVER feed a grizzly bear! Grizzly bears that have
been fed human food will wander farther into villages
and towns. Grizzly bears have been known to dig
through garbage bins and even break into people's
homes in search of food. Encounters with grizzlies
can be deadly for both humans and bears! Remember,
grizzly bears are best enjoyed from a distance.

GRIZZLY ETYMOLOGY

The word *grizzly* comes from the Middle English word
grizzle. Grizzle describes something having both light
and dark parts. A grizzly bear has both light hair and
dark hair—that's what makes it look brown!

CONVERTING SQUARE MILES TO ACRES

There are 640 square miles in one acre.

To convert square miles to acres:	To convert acres to square miles:
multiply the number of square miles by 640	divide the number of acres by 640

OM "NOM-NOM-NOM" NIVORE

Animals can be classified into groups by what they eat.

- Carnivores only eat meat. That meat comes from other animals! Carnivores have sharp teeth for tearing and cutting meat.

- Herbivores only eat plant material. Herbivores have flat teeth for grinding and chewing plants.

- Omnivores eat both meat and plants. Omnivores have some sharp teeth for tearing meat and some flat teeth for grinding plants.

Like humans, grizzly bears are omnivores. Grizzly bears will eat almost anything—dead or alive!

KNOW YOUR BEARS

Two different species of bears inhabit the contiguous United States: black bears and grizzly bears. Learn about the main differences between the two:

GRIZZLY BEAR

Front track

Front claw (2-4" long)

Dished face profile

Short, rounded ears

Shoulder hump

Long, light claws

BLACK BEAR

Front track

Front claw (1-2" long)

Straight face profile

Taller ears

No shoulder hump

Short, dark claws

TAKE YOUR GARBAGE AND MAKE A GARDEN

Composting is a way to turn household and yard waste into valuable food for plants! In this process, microorganisms in the soil eat organic waste and break it down to its simplest parts. This leads to a mineral-rich material called *humus* that can be used as fertilizer for plants.

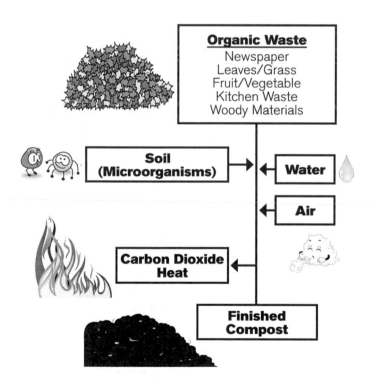

BEAR HIBERNATION

Hibernation is a way for animals to cope with the harsh winter when little food is available. Grizzly bears hibernate for about 5 months in the winter. During the summer and fall, grizzlies build up reserves of fat by eating as much as they can. In late fall or winter, the bears typically dig a hole on a hillside for their winter den. The den entrance is usually just big enough for the bear to squeeze through!

During hibernation, bears don't eat, drink, or even go to the bathroom! Their heart rate drops from about 50 beats per minute (bpm) to about 10 bpm. Pregnant female bears give birth in January or February, and care for the young cubs inside the den until spring. But don't try to sneak into a hibernating bear's den—experts say they can be easily awakened during hibernation!

YOU CAN COUNT ON OLD FAITHFUL

Old Faithful is the most famous geyser in Yellowstone National Park. It erupts approximately every 90 minutes. A geyser is a hot spring that is under pressure and finally erupts, sending a blast of water and steam into the air.

Geysers have a tube-like hole that reaches deep into the Earth's crust. The tube is filled with water. At the bottom of the tube lies molten rock, which heats the water in the tube. When the water gets hot enough, it begins to boil. The boiling water turns to gas, or steam, and shoots out of the tube and into the air. After the eruption, water slowly moves back into the tube, and the process begins again!

GLOSSARY

ambassador – an official representative of a country

ancestor – a person who was in someone's family in past times; a person from whom one is descended

camouflage – an adaptation of an animal to its environment that helps it blend in, increasing its chance of survival

conductor – a material that permits the flow of energy

dead ringer – a person or thing that closely resembles another

detour – a long or roundabout route taken to avoid something or to visit somewhere along the way

ecosystem – community of plants, animals, and smaller organisms that live, feed, reproduce, and interact in the same area or environment

endangered species – a species present in such small numbers that it is at risk of extinction

erode – to gradually destroy something, or to be gradually destroyed by natural forces such as water, wind, or ice

gall bladder – the small sac-shaped organ beneath the liver, in which bile is stored after secretion by the liver and before release into the intestine

geothermal – related to the internal heat of the Earth

grisly – causing a shudder or feeling of horror

habitat – the natural environment of a plant or animal

SAD **ingenious** – very smart or clever

inspiration – the process of being mentally stimulated to do something creative

insulator – any material that keeps energy such as electricity, heat, or cold from easily transferring through it

SAD **lustrous** – shiny; brilliant

maul – to physically attack and badly hurt a person or animal

microorganism – an organism too small to be seen with the unaided eye, like bacteria or protozoa

SAD **ominous** – giving the impression that something bad or unpleasant is going to happen

SAD **peripheral** – related to, or located on the edge of something

plantigrade – walking on the soles of the feet, like a human or a bear

SAD **pristine** – in its original condition; unspoiled

SAD **propel** – drive, push, or cause to move in a particular direction, typically forward

SAD **rogue** – behaving in ways that are not expected or not normal

SAD **sarcastic** – using words that mean the opposite of what you really want to say especially in order to insult someone, to show irritation, or to be funny

shambles – a state of total disorder

spawn – to cause something to develop or begin

wildlife biologist – a person who studies animals and their environment

Enjoy this exciting excerpt from:

THE MYSTERY AT

RATTLESNAKE

RIDGE

1

S-O-S

"I feel like I've stepped into a painting!" Avery cried.

"It's the most beautiful sight I've ever seen!" her younger sister Ella agreed, admiring the shades of salmon and blush pink in the late afternoon sky, and the bluebonnets that carpeted the landscape as far as she could see.

Moved by the brisk March wind, the bluebonnets bobbed their fancy heads like ladies in a fashion show. "No wonder this is the state flower of Texas," Avery said, stretching her arms and spreading her fingers for the wind to flow through them.

Ella carefully composed a picture in her camera's viewfinder. "It feels awesome get fresh air after being cooped up in the *Mystery Girl* for hours," she said, snapping the photo.

Avery, Ella, and their younger brother Evan were excited when Mimi and Papa invited them on a spring break trip to a cattle ranch near Sweetwater, Texas. As soon as Papa's little red plane landed, they bolted for the open spaces like rodeo bulls out of a chute. The trip from their grandparents' hometown of Palmetto Bluff, South Carolina, to "deep in the heart of Texas," took what felt like an eternity to three impatient kids.

The ranch owners, Gertie and Lilman Scott, had met Mimi and Papa a few years earlier after the *Mystery Girl* made an emergency landing on the airstrip behind their ranch house. In the days it took for the plane to be repaired, the four had formed solid friendships. When the Scotts invited them to bring their grandkids for a visit, Mimi eagerly agreed.

Mimi, a famous children's mystery writer, was always eager to introduce her grandkids to new sights and sounds. "Every trip is educational," she always said. Avery also knew her grandmother's head was like a blond sponge soaking up every experience for use in some future story or book. "I collect memories to weave into stories the way some grandmothers collect yarn to crochet colorful blankets," Mimi once told her.

Avery smiled as she remembered the discussion they'd had a few days before the trip.

"You've never seen wide open spaces like they have in Texas!" Mimi said as she flipped through her "T" encyclopedia to find pictures.

"Oh, Mimi!" Avery said, rolling her blue eyes and turning on her iPad. "No one uses encyclopedias anymore! Our teacher said we have to be comfortable using technology to live in the 21st century."

"Yep," Ella chimed in. "But *all* of STEM is important!"

"STEM?" Papa asked.

"It stands for Science, Technology, Engineering, and Math," Ella explained. "Those are the things we can use to solve the world's problems."

"Hmmm..." Papa said. "When I was a tadpole like you, we studied RRR."

"That sounds more like a growl than something you study!" Evan said, raising his hands to scratch the air like a snarling animal.

"It stands for Reading, Writing, and Arithmetic," Papa said.

"I guess that didn't include spelling," Ella muttered. "Only one of those things starts with 'r.'"

"We study the three 'R's' too," Evan said. "Only it stands for Reduce, Reuse, and Recycle. Those are things we have to do to keep the earth healthy."

In a flash, Avery found scads of information on the largest state in the lower 48 states. "Until the United States purchased Alaska from Russia in 1867, Texas was the largest state," she read. "Wow! It's 268,820 square miles!"

"Well, how many *round* miles is it?" Evan asked.

Avery looked at her little brother. "You can go on a round trip, Evan, but there's no such thing as round miles," she said. "You have to multiply the length times the width of something to find its area. The answer is always in square units—in this case, the units are miles."

"Avery!" Ella called, bringing her sister back to the present. "Look at this!" Ella was lying on her belly studying a buzzing bee hovering over a bluebonnet. "Each flower is actually a lot of tiny blooms growing on a central stalk."

"If that bee stings your nose, you're gonna look like an anteater," Avery teased.

"It's weird," Ella said, lost in her flower observation. "The bee is only visiting the blooms that have white in the center, and ignoring these at the bottom with purple in the center."

Avery was proud she had brought her iPad on the trip and had read about all things Texas during the flight, including bluebonnets.

"That's one of the plant's **adaptations** that help it survive," Avery explained. "The white spots are only on blooms that have recently opened. They have the freshest and best pollen on them. The white spots turn purple as the blooms get old and their pollen is no longer good and fresh. Since the bees are only attracted to the white spots, they don't waste their time collecting the bad pollen on the purple blooms. It helps the bees get plenty of good pollen to take back to their hives. It also helps the bluebonnets because they get pollinated by only the best pollen and can make lots of good bluebonnet seeds."

"That's cool!" Ella said, impressed with her sister's knowledge. "You're like a bluebonnet encyclopedia. Hey, Evan! Come and watch this busy bee!" Ella glanced around and suddenly realized her little brother was nowhere in sight. "Avery, where's Evan?" she asked.

"He's probably found an interesting rock that captured his attention," Avery replied.

Ella nodded. "Leave it to Evan to ignore all these beautiful wildflowers to look at a rock."

The girls jogged back to the top of the small ridge they'd crossed. Their long blond hair blew in the stiff breeze. "Wow!" Avery said, when she realized how far they'd come. Her **perspective** made the ranch house look small enough to fit on a Monopoly board.

"Yep, there he is, staring at a rock," Ella said, spotting her brother standing with his back toward them like he'd been tapped in a game of freeze tag.

"Evan, we better head back," Avery called. Evan didn't move. "Let's go, Evan!" she called again. Evan continued to stand still as a statue. "It's not funny, Evan! I know you're playing the stubborn game, but we really should get back to the ranch house before it gets dark!" Frustrated, Avery yelled, "OK! Stand there all night if you want. You can play chase with the coyotes!"

When Avery and Ella headed down the ridge, a sound made them stop. "Whee, Whee, Whee...WHEEEEEEEEEEEEEEEE, WHEEEEEEEEEEEE, WHEEEEEEEEEE... Whee, Whee, Whee."

"Is he whistling?" Avery asked.

"I think so," Ella said. "It sounds like that annoying thing he learned at camp last summer. Remember, he kept practicing until he almost drove us crazy."

Avery eyes grew wide. "You mean the SOS signal?"

"Yes, that," Ella said. "I can't remember what those letters stand for, but I think it means 'Help!'"

"Wait! He really might be in trouble," Avery said, trotting back up the ridge.

Seeing Evan's face confirmed Avery's fear. He was pale as a bowl of Mimi's grits and his bright blue eyes were as big as jawbreakers. As the girls got closer, they heard another sound that stopped them, puzzled, in their tracks. It was a steady s-s-s-s-s-s-s-s-s—like water spraying full blast, or the buzzing of a kid's wind-up toy. Cautiously moving only a finger, Evan pointed at the ground.

Avery and Ella gasped and stifled their screams with their hands!